VACATION SURPRISES

VACATION

written and illustrated by

ATHENEUM

SURPRISES

Patricia Montgomery Newton

New York   1986

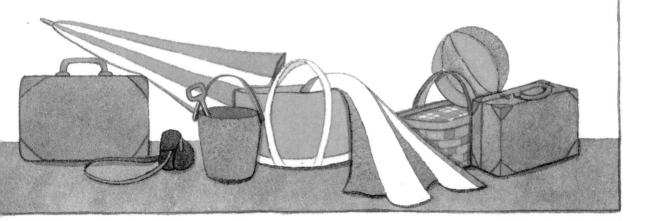

For Seth

Atheneum
Macmillan Publishing Company
866 Third Avenue, New York, NY 10022

Type set by Linoprint Composition, New York City
Printed and bound by the Toppan Printing Company, Inc., Japan
Typography by Mary Ahern

10   9   8   7   6   5   4   3   2   1

Library of Congress Cataloging-in-Publication Data

Newton, Patricia Montgomery.   Vacation surprises.

  SUMMARY: Pig friends Lily and Orlando look forward to a marvelous vacation but find a striking contrast between their plans and reality.
  [1. Pigs—Fiction.   2. Vacations—Fiction]   I. Title.
PZ7.N48695Vac   1986   [E]   86-3649
ISBN 0-689-31264-4

ONE fine summer morning Lily and Orlando
were packing to go on vacation.

"I will have a very exciting week in the mountains,"
said Lily, who was going camping.

"I prefer a relaxing week in the sun," said Orlando.
He was traveling to a seaside resort.

"Every morning I will get up at dawn," said Lily.

"And I will sleep until ten," said Orlando.

"I will catch a fish and fry it for breakfast,"
said Lily.

"And I will have tea and cinnamon toast on a tray
in bed," said Orlando.

"Then I will spend the day paddling my canoe,"
said Lily.

"While I take a long walk on the beach,"
said Orlando.

"I can't wait to climb to the top of the mountain,"
said Lily.

"I will sit on the sand and watch the waves roll in,"
said Orlando.

"Every night I will toast marshmallows over a campfire
and fall asleep under the stars," said Lily.

"And I will watch the sunset and write postcards to
my friends," said Orlando.

"Send one to me," said Lily, as she waved good-bye.

"Have a good trip," called Orlando.

On Monday morning Lily rose with the sun.

Orlando had breakfast in bed.
And lunch in bed. And dinner in bed.

On Tuesday Lily went fishing for breakfast.

While Orlando had tea and cinnamon toast on a tray again.

On Wednesday Lily paddled her canoe.

Orlando went for a walk on the beach.

On Thursday Lily climbed to the top of the mountain.

And Orlando sat on the sand and watched the waves.

On Friday Lily toasted marshmallows and watched the stars come out.

While Orlando watched the sunset and wrote postcards
to his friends.

On Saturday the two friends returned home.
"How was your vacation?" asked Lily.

"Surprisingly relaxing," answered Orlando. "How was your
vacation?"
"Surprisingly exciting," said Lily.